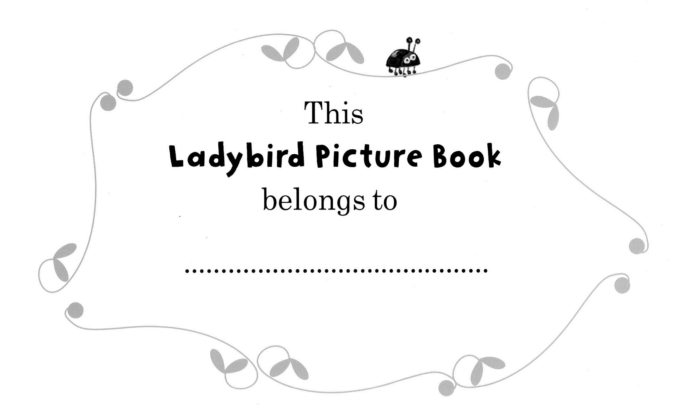

This
Ladybird Picture Book
belongs to

....

LADYBIRD BOOKS

UK | USA | Canada | Ireland | Australia
India | New Zealand | South Africa
Ladybird Books is part of the Penguin Random House group of companies
whose addresses can be found at global.penguinrandomhouse.com.

www.penguin.co.uk   www.puffin.co.uk   www.ladybird.co.uk

Penguin
Random House
UK

First published 2015
This Ladybird Picture Books edition published 2019
001

Copyright © Ladybird Books Ltd, 2015, 2019

Printed in China
A CIP catalogue record for this book is available from the British Library

ISBN: 978–0–241–38428–2

All correspondence to:
Ladybird Books, Penguin Random House Children's
80 Strand, London WC2R 0RL

Ladybird Picture Books

Alice in Wonderland

BASED ON THE CLASSIC TALE BY LEWIS CARROLL

retold by Ronne Randall ★ illustrated by Ailie Busby

One hot summer's day, Alice and her sister
sat under a tree. Alice's sister opened a book.
Alice leaned over to take a look.

"No pictures!" she said.
"It's boring!"
She closed her eyes
in the shade of the tree.

Alice woke up. She saw a flash of white fur.
A rabbit in a jacket was rushing past her.
"Oh, dear!" he said. "I'm late, I'm late!"

Alice jumped up. "A talking rabbit, wearing clothes!" she said. "I'll follow him and see where he goes!"

The White Rabbit darted down a hole in the ground. Alice scampered after him.

Down she tumbled.

Down, down,
down she fell.

Until she landed at the bottom
with a great big BUMP,
hitting the ground with
a thumpety THUMP!

Alice could see a tiny door, but to reach it
she had to lie on the floor.
It was locked. Alice saw a key on the table.
"I will use that to open the door."

Then she saw a bottle marked 'Drink Me'.
"If I drink this potion, perhaps it will shrink me."
Alice drank the potion.

Now she was too small,
the key was too high!

Alice suddenly noticed a cake beside her.
"That will make me grow!" she said. "Here I go!"
But the cake made her too big.

The next minute, the walls and the door were gone.
There Alice stood, looking out at a beautiful wood.

The White Rabbit had gone. All Alice could see was a Cheshire Cat grinning high up in a tree.

"Maybe the White Rabbit went to see the March Hare," said the cat, pointing. "He lives just over there."

There was a tea party going on at the March Hare's house. He had invited his friends the Mad Hatter and the Dormouse.

The Mad Hatter was noisy and full of chatter,
but the Dormouse had fallen fast asleep!

With no sign of the White Rabbit,
Alice decided to stay and have some tea.

The Mad Hatter was all of a-flutter because
he had found some crumbs in the butter.
"It was the best butter!" said the March Hare.

Alice decided she'd had enough
of all this silly, silly stuff.
She came to a garden.
"What a strange sight," she said.
The gardeners were painting
the white roses red!

All at once the White Rabbit appeared.
He blew a trumpet, and a queen dressed in red
marched up and shouted, "Off with her head!"

"This is MY garden – I am the Queen of Hearts.
You don't belong here!"

Alice said, "You're just a pack of cards!
I'm not scared of you!"
The pack of cards flew up into the air.

Alice quickly opened her eyes.
She looked all around.
She was back with her sister, safe and sound.

"You've had such a long sleep,"
her sister cried.
"And such a strange dream!"
Alice quietly replied.
And she told her sister all about it.

Ladybird Picture Books

Look out for...

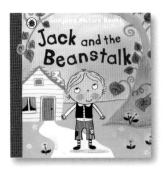 Jack and the Beanstalk

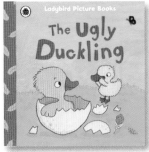 The Ugly Duckling

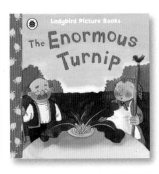 The Enormous Turnip

 Chicken Licken

 The Three Little Pigs

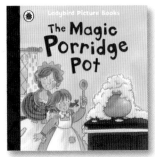 The Magic Porridge Pot

 The Sly Fox and the Little Red Hen

 Hansel and Gretel

 Cinderella

 Goldilocks and the Three Bears

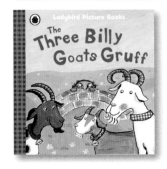 The Three Billy Goats Gruff

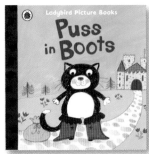 Puss in Boots

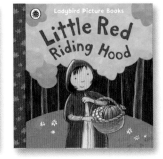 Little Red Riding Hood

 The Wizard of Oz

 The Little Red Hen

 The Gingerbread Man

 Alice in Wonderland

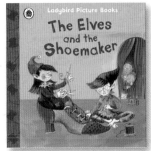 The Elves and the Shoemaker